I See a Cat

PAUL MEISEL

I Like to Read®

HOLIDAY HOUSE • NEW YORK

I Like to Read® books, created by award-winning
picture book artists as well as talented newcomers,
instill confidence and the joy of reading in new readers.

We want to hear every new reader say, "I like to read!"

Visit our website for flashcards and activities:
www.holidayhouse.com/I-Like-to-Read/
#ILTR
This book has been tested by an educational expert
and determined to be a guided reading level A.

I LIKE TO READ is a registered trademark of Holiday House, Inc.

Copyright © 2017 by Paul Meisel
All Rights Reserved
HOLIDAY HOUSE is registered in the U.S. Patent and Trademark Office.
Printed and bound in March 2018 at Worzalla, Stevens, Point, WI, USA.
The artwork was created with watercolor, acrylic and pencil on
Strathmore paper with digital enhancement.
www.holidayhouse.com
First Edition
3 5 7 9 10 8 6 4 2

Library of Congress Cataloging-in-Publication Data is available.

ISBN 978-0-8234-3680-4 (hardcover)
ISBN 978-0-8234-3849-5 (paperback)

For Marcia, Tim and Jeanne,
dog lovers all

I see a cat.

I see a bird.

I see a fly.

I see a squirrel.

I see mice.

I see a bee.

I see a squirrel.

I see a boy.

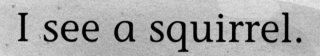

I see a squirrel.